Parthenium's Year

Stan C. Smith

Parthenium's Year

This is a work of fiction. All the characters and events portrayed in this book are either products of the author's imagination or are used fictitiously.

Copyright © 2017 Stan C. Smith
All rights reserved.
ISBN-13: 978-1979247399
ISBN-10: 1979247390

"A wise lover values not so much the gift of the lover as the love of the giver."

— Thomas à Kempis, The Imitation of Christ (written 1418-1427)

JUNE

Spencer Wolfe was tired of choices. Junk food packages with neon-primary colors hung in rows before him. Too damned many choices. He shook his head and plucked a bag of Chile Picante Corn Nuts from its hanger on the endcap. He then walked to the glass wall of cooler doors where there were hundreds of different bottled drinks to choose from.

A girl stood there, looking through the glass at the Cokes. She had long, sand-colored hair and wore frayed cutoff jean shorts like she was from one of those old TV shows. But her legs looked athletic, and this made Spencer's decision easier—he would get a Coke. He stopped next to the girl and gazed at the array of personalized plastic bottles, each with a different name on it.

"What's your name," he asked. "Maybe I can help you spot it."

The girl glanced at him but didn't smile, probably not a good sign. "What's in a name, anyway?"

Spencer looked at her again. That was an odd response. He decided to take a chance. "That which we call a rose, by any other name would smell as sweet."

This time she looked at him. She was cute, for a townie.

Spencer said, "Is your name Rose? If it is, I bet we can find one." He nodded toward the Coke bottles.

"You won't find my name in there," she said.

"Okay, then what is it?"

She seemed to think about this like it was a hard question. Then she said, "Kiss a lover, dance a measure, find your name, and buried treasure."

Spencer stared at her. "Okay."

She continued gazing at him, and it started getting uncomfortable. Finally, she smiled slightly. "When I was eight, I found a young box turtle." She held her fingers apart a few inches to show the turtle's size. "I was quite taken with it immediately. But I knew I should let it go. I set it on the ground and it started to walk away. I said, 'Turtle, do you have a name?' It didn't reply. So I said, 'I like the name Scuttles. When I see you again, I'll call you Scuttles.' But then it was too late. I knew the turtle's name. So I took it home with me."

Spencer waited, but the girl just smiled. "So what happened then?"

"Scuttles changed my life. It was twelve years ago, and I still have him today. I will finally let him go this year."

"Are you afraid I'll take you home with me if you tell me your name?"

She actually giggled a little at this. "I have bigger things to be afraid of. Besides, fear doesn't shut you down; it wakes you up." She then put a hand over her mouth as if realizing Spencer was becoming confused. "I'm sorry. I read a lot. Do you really want to know? No one has ever asked me my name."

"You're kidding, right?" When she didn't respond, Spencer said, "Well, I'm happy to be the first."

She looked around like she was about to reveal a secret. "Parthenium."

Was she serious? Parthenium? But then Spencer recalled something. "Wait, I think I know your sister, Dalea. I met her once when I was home from Drury. Is she your sister? Are you a Templeton?"

The girl's demeanor changed. She looked down at her feet. "I should probably go."

"I'm sorry. Did I say something wrong? I was just making conversation."

Parthenium seemed to hesitate. "Okay," she said. Then she stood there, looking at him.

Spencer opened the cooler door. "Wait a second." He located a bottle with the name, Spencer, and one with the name, Rose. "How about if I buy you a Coke, and we can talk some more outside? We could walk if you want." He thought it might seem weird if he asked her to go for a ride in his car.

She agreed to this, and soon they left the Mini Mart convenience store and began walking down Boone Street. There weren't many sidewalks in Oak Green, Missouri, so they walked on the street.

Spencer wanted to know more about her, but he decided to be cautious. "My family moved here when I was in fifth grade, so I kind of grew up here. But I've been at Drury U in Springfield for five years, so I haven't been around much. Maybe that's why I haven't met you before?"

Parthenium nodded at this but didn't speak.

"I graduated a few weeks ago, so I just moved back home. Now I have to figure out what I'm going to do with a business marketing degree. There are too many choices, and right now I'm burned out."

Again she just nodded.

"I'm sorry," Spencer said. "I should just shut up and let you talk."

She glanced at him. "Conversations consist for the most part of things one does not say."

"Is that you speaking, or something you've read?"

They arrived at 14th Street and she pointed to the right. "May we walk this way? I enjoy seeing the houses." They turned the corner. "I would like to say more to you, but I haven't had much experience talking to strangers."

"Have you been hiding somewhere all your life?"

She looked down at her feet again. "Well maybe, if that's what you consider being home-schooled. Mostly I've talked to my siblings. And my mother." She walked for some seconds in silence, and Spencer decided to shut up, to see if she would continue. Finally, she spoke again. "You were right. I am a Templeton. My mother home-schools all of us."

"All of you? How many of you are there?"

Parthenium frowned at this. "I'd rather not say. Will you tell me more about your family?"

"Well, I'm back living with my mom now. She teaches second grade over at Butler County R3. No brothers or sisters. Dad and mom divorced, and he lives over in West Plains. He's a welder. Works for a plant that makes military trucks, or some shit like that."

She made a face when he said that.

"I'm sorry. You don't like that word?"

She seemed to think about this. "When my brother, Castor, was about four, he came into the house carrying feces in his hand. I don't know if it was his or from the dog, but he had taken a bite of it. Instead of shouting at him, my mother took him to the kitchen and pointed at some blackberries, tomatoes, and other produce from the garden. She asked, 'Why would you eat that poop when you have so many better choices available?'"

Spencer waited and then realized her story was done. He smiled. "You do know how to make a point. You're an interesting girl, Parthenium."

She shook her head and smiled just slightly. "I've never really met anyone outside of my family, so I can't say if you are interesting or just average. Perhaps other boys are much more interesting than you."

He laughed. "For my sake, I'm going to assume that's a joke."

They walked a few more blocks and then turned around. By the time they returned to the Mini Mart, Spencer had decided this was the strangest conversation he'd ever had. But it was also the best time he'd had in weeks.

When they got to his Malibu, he slapped the car's roof. "Well, this is me."

"It looks nothing like you," she said.

He snorted. "If anyone else said that, it would just be sad. Somehow you make it work."

"That's good, I suppose." She shuffled her sandals on the pavement. "Do you know you haven't told me your name?"

"I'm sorry. I'm Spencer Wolfe."

She looked at him for a moment. "Are you going to change my life, Spencer Wolfe?"

"I could ask you the same thing. Do you think I could see you again?"

She hesitated. "My father died before I was born. My mother tells me he was an exceptional man. She met him when she was sixteen. She was working at a craft and produce stand on Highway 142 outside of Poplar Bluff. My father had just graduated high school and he was traveling with no destination in mind. He stopped at my mother's stand. There weren't any other customers there, so they talked. There was chemistry, as they say. But finally, other customers came, and my father decided it was time to leave. He bought a basket of peaches, shook my mother's hand, and went to his car. He started his car, and then my mother picked up another peach and ran to him. She told him his basket was short one peach. He turned off his car and sat there eating his extra peach while she helped the other customers. When she was alone again, he got out of his car and came back to her."

Parthenium smiled at Spencer. "For as long as I can remember, my mother has said to me and all of my siblings, 'An extra peach won't hurt you.'"

Spencer wasn't sure, but he thought maybe this was her way of saying yes. "I don't have a peach," he said. He then took her hand and held it palm up. He placed the crinkled, half-empty bag he'd been carrying into her hand. "How do you feel about corn nuts?"

∞

When Spencer got home his mom was already there. It was her last day with students before the summer break, and Spencer knew she'd be tired, but she was making fried chicken anyway. She wouldn't be doing that if he were still at Drury.

"Jesus, Mom, I could have made something. I should have come home sooner."

She just smiled and pushed her hair from her face with flour-white fingers. "I'm still just thrilled you're here, Spence. Two months from now, maybe it'll be different."

Spencer sat on one of the stools at the kitchen island to watch her cook, like he had done when he was a kid. "Don't worry, I'll get a job by then."

She opened her paper bag of flour and chicken pieces and started arranging them in the hot oil in her cast iron skillet. "Doesn't that process involve filling out applications?" Her tone was clear even over the sizzling pan.

Spencer's lofty mood precluded such a frustrating topic, so he ignored this. "I met an interesting girl. Actually, interesting is an understatement."

His mom paused what she was doing. "Alright, well played. You have my attention."

"I've never met anyone like her. Her name's Parthenium. She's a Templeton. Remember the Templetons? They have that huge property off CC road."

Spencer watched his mom carefully as he said this, and he saw her shoulders slump. He'd been afraid of that. The Templetons had somewhat of a strange reputation in Oak Green—probably throughout the whole county. All Spencer knew was what his buddies in high school used to say, that they were a family of hillbillies with lots of kids, and no one knew who the fathers were for any of them. They lived in a big house on something like four hundred acres, but Spencer had no idea how they got their money.

He waited, and finally his mom asked, "Parthenium, did you say? Interesting name. That's wild quinine."

"Wild quinine?"

She turned to glance at him. "It's a plant. Mrs. Templeton's name is Viola, the name for violets. The girls in the family seem to be named after wildflowers—Viola's folks were hippies, I guess. I believe one of the girls was your age. Dalea, I think. The name for prairie clover."

"Yeah, Dalea," he said. "What do you mean, she *was*?"

Again she glanced at him. "She died while you were at Drury. About three years ago."

Spencer's chest suddenly tightened. "What? We talked about Dalea today! She didn't tell me that." But he recalled Parthenium's response when he had mentioned Dalea. "Jesus, no wonder she didn't want to talk about it."

His mom put the last chicken piece in the pan and adjusted the burner's knob. She came over to the island and sat across from him. "You might want to know something else. About two years ago, another sister died. Her name was Trillium. They were both about twenty when they died."

"Spencer stared at her. "How did they die?"

She shrugged. "Inconclusive."

"What does that mean?"

"It means no one knows. If I recall, the autopsies were inconclusive. Foul play was ruled out, thank God. But beyond that, well, they just died."

Spencer gazed down at his hands resting on the island. "What the hell?"

"Watch your mouth, Spence. My house, my rules."

Spencer rolled his eyes, but for a moment he considered what words might be better choices. "What do you know about the Templetons? I've heard a few things, but not much."

She sighed. "Turn the chicken over, would you?" She then left the room.

A few minutes later she was back. She placed a delicate object the size of a plate on the island. It was fragile-looking and was constructed of thin, white fish bones. And Spencer had always thought it was beautiful.

"My sin sucker?"

She smiled at this. "Son, you're the only one who calls them that. The Templetons call them sin swallowers. At least that's what they were calling them when we bought yours, and when your grammie and grandpa bought mine."

"Okay," Spencer said as he picked it up to examine it. "Now you have *my* attention."

"The Templetons make these. They have for a long time. They're the only ones who do make them—only ones who ever have. But several generations ago they did something else. They were sin eaters. They actually got paid to do that."

Spencer had heard about sin eaters. It was an old Ozark tradition. Maybe in other places, too. When someone died, the family asked the sin eater to come. They would place a plate of food on the dead person's chest. The food would soak up all the sins of the deceased. Then the sin eater would eat the plate of food, freeing the person's soul from the sins. Or something like that.

He asked, "Do people still hire sin eaters?"

She shrugged. "I doubt it. That's why the Templetons don't do it anymore. Back in the forties, people began to think of it as old-fashioned. So the Templetons changed with the times. They started making sin swallowers instead, which worked out pretty well for them. Everyone around here thought there was something strange about the Templeton land. The spring water, specifically. Allegedly, their spring was contaminated with something strange, perhaps something magical, and drinking the water from their spring was what made the Templetons good sin eaters. So they started making sin swallowers out of things that lived in the water, or near it. Yours is made from bones of fish that lived in the spring. Somehow they convinced people that everyone needed to have their own sin swallower, especially newborn babies. People bought them and hung them up over the crib to swallow all the child's sins." She made quotation marks in the air as she said the last few words.

Spencer gazed at his sin sucker. He hadn't seen it in years. "You have one of these, too?"

"Sure do. And your dad has one. For several generations, everyone in this area would buy them whenever they were expecting a child. Some babies would have several because people gave them as gifts. People still buy them, although now I'm sure they just use them for decoration, kind of like dream catchers.

He set it back down. "So the Templetons make sin suckers. That's a little weird. But whatever."

She went back to the stove to turn the chicken pieces again and spoke over her shoulder. "Well, I told you that to give you some context. Back in the day, people made a habit of avoiding sin eaters. They were afraid all those sins they consumed might take over. So people pretty much shunned the Templetons and their land. A reputation like that doesn't go away easily. Still today, even though people buy their sin swallowers, they badmouth the Templetons. And it doesn't help that the family seems to have so many secrets. And then when the girls died...." She just shook her head instead of finishing this thought.

Spencer sighed and stood up. "Well thanks, Mom. Now I've had two really weird conversations in one day."

"Do you think you'll see this Parthenium girl again?" she asked without turning around.

"Yes, indeed I will. I'm seeing her tomorrow, in fact. With any luck, you'll soon have some grandchildren."

She let out a loud laugh. "Finally! And I imagine we'll get a discount on sin swallowers for each of them." She then turned to him without a smile on her face. "Son, I trust you know what you're doing."

He shook his head. "Since the day I graduated, I've had no idea what I'm doing."

∞

Spencer sat at a picnic table at the north end of Rotary Park, waiting for Parthenium and looking at the graffiti and initials carved into the table. It was a ridiculous situation. He was twenty-three, and he was waiting for a date in the park next to the swimming pool. He was pretty sure he had done the exact same thing when he was in eighth grade.

A white four-door Wrangler pulled up behind his Malibu, and Parthenium climbed out of it. She flashed a smile before leaning back into the Jeep to get something, and suddenly the park seemed like a fine place to meet.

PARTHENIUM'S YEAR

Spencer's heart quickened as she sat next to him instead of choosing the opposite bench. She placed a brown paper bag on the picnic table. She leaned on her elbows and gazed at his face, her eyes roaming over every inch of it as if she had never seen a face before.

Spencer decided to wait, to see what she might say first. But it seemed she was much more comfortable with the silence than he was.

"I'm glad you came," he said. "I was beginning to wonder."

"I'm sorry about that. I made something for you this morning. It took some time. I hope you like it." She pushed the paper bag in front of him.

He picked it up. "You made something for me?"

She scooted a little closer on the bench, obviously excited. "For so many centuries, the exchange of gifts has held us together. It has made it possible to bridge the abyss where language struggles."

He looked at her. "Part of why I like you is that I never know what you're going to say next." He opened the bag and pulled out a flat box, about eight inches square and only an inch tall, with a clear plastic lid. Behind the plastic was white cotton, and pressed between the cotton and the lid was a beautiful object, apparently made mostly from transparent wings of some large insect and held together by a circular wire frame.

"Take it out of the box," she said, almost giggling. "I'll show you how it works."

Spencer removed the lid and carefully lifted the item out. The insect wings were arranged in an overlapping spiral, with a hole in the middle that was spanned by one very large wing. When he held it up, sunlight poured through the wings, producing dozens of tiny multi-colored rainbows on the picnic table.

"Parthenium, this is amazing!"

"Those are dragonfly wings," she said, pointing to the overlapping spiral. "The lens in the center is from a cicada. I made it so you can look through it."

He raised the object to his eye and looked at her through the center opening. The wing's membrane distorted her face, and the web of thin veins made her look like slightly dislodged pieces of a jigsaw puzzle. It was mesmerizing, and everything around her seemed to fade to nothing, allowing him to focus only on her surreal image.

He lowered the creation from his face. "I don't know what to say. I've never seen anything like it."

She smiled and made a cute gesture of raising her shoulders like she was pleased. "Spencer, you and I are beginning a new story. A story is a butterfly whose wings transport us to another world. One where we receive gifts that change who we are and who we want to be."

He still didn't know what to say, so he just shook his head.

"I don't have a name for it, really," she said. "But I can tell you what it's for. When things get confusing—when too many choices are before you—look through it. It will help you focus on only one choice at a time. That's what you need to do, you know. When people will not weed their own minds, they are apt to be overrun by nettles."

He put it to his eye again, this time focusing beyond her, on her car. He rotated the object slowly, and the puzzle pieces moved about as if the Jeep were a Transformer. At that moment, everything but the Jeep itself seemed blurred and unimportant. He then carefully put it back in its box.

"When I first saw it, I thought you were giving me my second sin swallower."

She put a hand to her mouth to stifle a laugh. "You have one of those?"

"Since I was a baby. My mom got it out yesterday when I told her you were a Templeton."

Her smile faded and she looked at the tabletop. "I imagine you talked about my family."

"Only because I'd like to know more about you."

She seemed to consider this. Finally, she said, "I have a younger sister, Helianthus. When she was seven and I was thirteen, my mother got a goat for me to raise. Helianthus took a liking to the poor thing. I was concerned about her age, and I told her the goat was a pet, that it was there just to eat the weeds from our yard. She gave it a name, and I didn't stop her. On the day I butchered the goat, Helianthus cried. And she cried the next day and the day after that. My mother told me that if I had told her the truth, and all of the truth, she would not have suffered like that."

Spencer waited, but the story had ended. He said, "So... you've decided to tell me all of the truth?"

Her eyes flicked up from the tabletop to meet his. "Too little of the truth can cause suffering. Too much of the truth can cause even worse."

"Okay, you decide where to draw the line. Yesterday I told you I knew Dalea. But you didn't tell me she had passed away. And you didn't mention that you had another sister who passed away. Trillium?"

She nodded slowly. "Yes, Trillium."

"I'm so sorry," he said. "That must have been terrible."

One corner of her mouth turned up slightly, a subtle acknowledgment. "I have a lot of siblings."

Was that a joke? Spencer decided to change the subject. "You know, you told me you were home-schooled, and that you haven't met many other people before. How is it that you lived your whole life like that, but now you come here into town two days in a row?"

Suddenly she got up and sat on the tabletop with her feet on the bench next to Spencer. She cradled her chin with her elbows on her knees. "I turned twenty, that's how. Now it's time for me to go out and do something great for the world."

Spencer watched for signs that she was joking but saw none. "Well, then you and I are kind of in the same boat."

"That's why I made your gift for you," she said. "You also must decide how you will make the world a better place."

He shook his head. "Maybe. But I think the world is pretty screwed up."

She actually put her hand on his. "So do all who live to see such times. But that is not for them to decide. All we have to decide is what to do with the time that is given us."

He turned his hand over and gripped hers. "I know that one! Gandalf said that, right?"

∞

At Spencer's request, Parthenium pulled her Jeep onto the grass shoulder of CC road, across the road from a brown sign that said *Coon Island Conservation Area – 3 miles*. Less than fifty yards ahead of them was a mailbox that said *Templeton*, next to a long driveway that wound back through the forest and out of sight. Spencer had caught glimpses of the house through the bare trees in winter, but now the forest was a solid green wall.

She sat behind the wheel, glancing at him occasionally.

"I'm sorry," he said. "I just need time to prepare myself."

"I'm in no hurry," she said. "The sun and moon aren't either. Nobody goes faster than the legs they have."

He sighed. "Does everyone in your family talk the way you do?"

She smiled at this. "You're asking what I would like you to witness for yourself. May I remind you that no sibling of mine has ever brought a boy into our home? You are the first, and so maybe I should be the one to be nervous."

He sighed again and stared at the mailbox.

Parthenium started tapping the steering wheel, and then she began singing.

"For Adam never had no mammy
for to take him on her knee,
to teach him right from wrong and
show him things he ought to see.
I know down in my heart he'd a
left that apple be,
but Adam never had no dear old
mammy."

Spencer was now sitting up straight. "You didn't tell me you could sing! That song's kind of old-timey, but your voice is amazing."

She blushed and shook her head slightly. "My siblings each have one specialty subject, but I have three. Music is one of them. My focus is Ozark folk music. Because, well...." She gestured toward the forest and hills surrounding them.

Her voice was still echoing in Spencer's mind. He wanted to hear more of it. "Do you know other songs, too?"

"Hundreds. They're all kind of obscure. Like I said, it's one of my specialty subjects." She began singing again.

"My little sister's seven.
She's sweet as she can be,
and as pretty as the picture on the wall.
The doctor came this summer,
and said that she would die,
when the autumn leaves begin to fall.

Won't you help me, mister,
please help me tie the leaves.
We'll tie them to the branches good and strong,
and if we tie them tightly,
my sister will not die,
and we'll show the doctor then that he was wrong."

She stopped singing and the Jeep became very quiet. Spencer didn't trust his own voice to speak without faltering.

"That one was collected in Benton County, Arkansas in 1960," Parthenium said softly.

Spencer cleared his throat before attempting to speak. "With that voice, you could sing professionally."

"I don't know," she said. "I doubt there are many people interested in old Ozark folk songs. And I don't have time to learn a new specialty subject."

Spencer frowned at this. "You're twenty years old. You have plenty of time."

She shook her head again. "How soon hath time, the subtle thief of youth, stolen on his wing my twentieth year." She then turned and met his gaze. "I will turn twenty-one in ten months. That's how long I have to do something important, to make the world a better place. You think I'm kidding, of course, but I am not. It is the way of my family. It is how things are, whether I think they should be or not. You leave the house when you turn

PARTHENIUM'S YEAR   17

twenty, you improve the world before you turn twenty-one."

Spencer started to speak, but she went on.

"My oldest sister, Cirsium, she was the one who set this standard. It wasn't the way of things when she turned twenty, but that year she changed our family business. She computerized everything for the first time. Now someone in Norway can buy a sin swallower if they have a mind to. And then Iris, she turned twenty, and she wrote a book of poetry before she was twenty-one. And then my brother Tamias, he wrote a three-hundred-page book on Ozark folk legends. And then Dalea—you knew Dalea—she specialized in music. She recorded an entire CD of original songs during her year. And then my sister, Trillium, also specialized in music. She recorded a CD of country and western songs during her year. She played and recorded all the instruments herself. And last year Mertensia turned twenty. She specialized in entrepreneurism and had three different products ready by her twentieth birthday. She then went to Little Rock and found investors to set up production. Her products started selling before she turned twenty-one."

Parthenium gripped the steering wheel tightly. "And now it's my turn. So no, I really don't have plenty of time. I am *expected* to accomplish something in the next ten months."

This was more than Spencer had ever heard her say at once, so he waited to be sure she was finished. "Maybe I can help you," he said. "I don't seem to have much planned for the next ten months. I mean, if you want my help."

She turned and gazed at him. Her expression made him wish he could freeze the moment and live in it forever.

She said, "Time is too slow for those who wait, too swift for those who fear, too long for those who grieve, too short for those who rejoice, but for those who love, time is eternity."

Was she telling him she loved him? On their third date? Spencer realized he hoped she was.

"Okay," he said. "So where do we start?"

She wiped moisture from one eye with her thumb. "We start right there," she said, and she pointed to the driveway beside the mailbox.

∞

The house was a three-story behemoth that could pass for a mansion if it had been built in a city. Behind it and a ways up the side of a hill was the original two-story stone house, which itself was an impressive structure.

Parthenium parked the Jeep in front of the newer house. There appeared to be no garage, and no other vehicles were to be seen.

"We use the stone house for our school," she said. "My mother doesn't allow us to bring school-related work to the new house, so most of my siblings will be in the school. My mother will probably be in the house." She raised her eyebrows at Spencer. "Are you ready for this, or do you need more time?"

Spencer stared at the house. Why was he so uptight? Perhaps because he was the first person ever to be invited here, that's why. "Are you sure this is a good idea?"

"Do you trust me?" she said.

He considered this. "This is the third time we've been together, but yeah, I do."

"Good, because when I met you I knew you would change my life, and I was pretty sure I would change yours. Do you want to hear another story?"

"Sure." Anything to delay going into that house.

"Please be very sure, because this story, once told, cannot be untold."

He frowned at her. "I'm sure."

Parthenium inhaled deeply and let it out. "My mother knows how to love. She loves like no person I have ever read about, and I read a lot. She met my father when she was sixteen, married him when she was seventeen, and he died when she was eighteen. Two years—that's all the time they had together. But compressed into those two years was a lifetime's worth of love. My mother had a baby girl just before my father died. He had only one week to love his daughter, my sister Cirsium." She paused.

"You okay?"

She nodded and went on. "My mother was heartbroken, but with Cirsium, she had a reason to go on living. She moved back here to the family property. She gave up my father's name, Dailey, and went back to the Templeton name so she could carry on the family business. The business was struggling then because my grandparents could make only two sin swallowers per week.

Parthenium turned the Jeep's key enough to lower the electric windows to let in fresh air. She looked at Spencer. "Are you sure you want to hear this?"

"I'm sure," he said. "Although I'm curious about why you refer to this man as your father."

She sighed. "During the two years my mother and father were together, his favorite place to take her was the state park up at Johnson's Shut-Ins. Three months after he died, my mother put Cirsium in her car and took my father's ashes up to the state park. She carried Cirsium and the ashes up to Horseshoe Glade. It was my father's favorite spot because he could look out across the St. Francois Mountains. She poured his ashes on the ground. She came back and tried to carry on with her life here. My mother was just a girl then, and my grandparents helped her care for Cirsium so she could make sin swallowers and sell them."

Parthenium glanced at Spencer. "A few months after taking my father's ashes up to Johnson's Shut-Ins, my mother realized she was pregnant. My sister, Iris, was born in April, one year after Cirsium's birth."

Now Spencer was starting to realize why she was reluctant to tell this story. "A year after your mother's husband died," he said.

"Exactly."

"Do you know who the father was?"

Parthenium held up one finger, indicating the question could wait. "My grandparents helped care for Cirsium and Iris. In July, three months after Iris was born, my mother went back up to the state park, to be close to my father's ashes." She glanced at him again. "You must understand that she loved him in a way most people could hardly imagine. The following April she gave birth to my brother, Tamias."

Again she held up a finger, even though Spencer hadn't spoken.

"And that July she went back again to be close to my father. My sister, Dalea, was born the following April. This continued. The following April, Trillium was born. The April after that, Mertensia. And the next April, I was born."

She stopped talking and watched him, perhaps waiting for a reaction.

"Um, did she ever tell you who the father is? Or the fathers?"

"I'm not sure you are hearing me," she said. "In July of each year, she went up to the state park to visit my father's gravesite. To talk to him. To tell him she still loved him. To lay on the ground at Horseshoe Glade where she had poured his ashes and touch the soil with her own hands, crying as she did so. She did not go up there to see another man." Spencer had no idea how to respond to this, so he kept his mouth shut.

She went on. "My mother was sick the summer after I was born, and she could not go visit my father's gravesite. She did not have a child that year. It was the only year she didn't. Every year after that she visited the place, and every April she gave birth to another child. Perilla, Helenium, Dasypus, Lotus, Helianthus, Didelphis, Castor, Justicia, Myotis, Ursus, Verbena, Matelea, Zizia, Silene, Alliaria, and then Delphinium, who is now three years old. Twenty-three of us in all, Spencer."

Again she watched him, waiting.

He cleared his throat. "You were right. That story cannot be untold."

"I'm not finished yet," she said. "My mother loves me and my siblings as fiercely as she loved my father. The people in Oak Green have not exactly been kind to my family over the years. And so my mother has always been protective of us—overprotective, most people would say. She does not allow any of us to leave the property."

"Until you turn twenty," Spencer said.

"Yes. And even then, it's not easy for her. And so this is not something to be taken lightly. It is not an opportunity to be wasted. My siblings prepare for it for years. They read, they study, and they practice. My mother spends a great deal of money on whatever they need for their specialty subjects. Computers, instruments, recording equipment, building materials, ingredients—whatever they need. So that they will be ready on their twentieth birthday."

She sighed loudly and stared through the windshield at the house. "I'm different from my siblings because I've never really known what I was going to do with this time. But now it's my turn, and I've decided my time involves you, Spencer. If you really want to help me, as you've said, you need to know the truth about my family." She reached for his hand and held it tight. "My answer is yes."

"Yes?"

"You asked if I was sure this is a good idea. My answer is yes." After a moment of silence, she snorted a loud laugh. "I imagine you think I'm strange. But how would I know what normal is?"

He studied her face. She was strange, perhaps the strangest person he had ever met—and the most wonderful. "I wish I could think of a perfect quote for this moment."

She puckered her lips in thought. "Not only is the universe stranger than we think, it is stranger than we *can* think."

Spencer nodded. He squeezed her hand tighter and turned to look up the hill at the stone house—the school. There were nine windows on the front of it, and in every window, at least one face stared back at him. Some of them were smaller, positioned in the lower panes of the windows. Others were older, looking out through the top panes. He waved. Three or four of the younger kids waved back.

"People who are late are often much jollier than people who have to wait for them."

Spencer jumped, startled by the new voice. It was Parthenium's mom. It had to be. She looked to be in her forties, although somewhat weathered and weary, like most of the rural women around here. Her hair was long and straight, and not styled in any particular way. She held a toddler in her arms, and she was walking up to Parthenium's side of the Jeep.

Parthenium spoke first. "Sorry, mother. We were talking. Trying to decide if this is a good idea after all."

The woman looked past Parthenium at Spencer. "He's already here, girl. That's like killing the chicken for meat and then deciding you'd rather have eggs."

Spencer extended a hand in front of Parthenium's face. "It's a pleasure to meet you, Mrs. Templeton, or Viola if you prefer. And I take it this might be Delphinium?" She smiled at him but didn't shake his hand or answer his question. "Why don't you two come inside? Lotus made blackberry cordial for the occasion." She turned and went back into the house.

As they walked to the front door, Spencer saw that they were still being watched from the windows of the school. They passed through a small foyer where black rubber mud boots lined each wall, arranged from small to large, and entered what could only be called a sitting room. The chairs were tasteful antiques, and there was no television or other electronics. Hanging on the walls were no fewer than ten sin swallowers. Some of them were made from fish bones, similar to Spencer's, but others were made from bird feathers and various dried vines, leaves, or roots. They were all beautiful. Parthenium sat on a floral-patterned couch with dark wood trim and motioned for him to sit beside her.

She spoke softly. "I should warn you, my mother doesn't believe in wasting time."

Viola entered the room carrying a tray with three tall glasses on it. "Lotus is caring for Delphinium so that we can talk." She handed them their drinks and sat down.

Spencer's glass contained purple juice with blackberries and green leaves floating amongst the ice cubes. He took a drink. It did not contain alcohol. "This is very good," he said.

Viola smiled at him again. "I don't know if you are aware of this, but Parthenium is a lover. Like I am."

Spencer shifted on the couch and glanced at Parthenium, who was watching him. "Ma'am, I'm not sure how to respond to that."

"That response is fine," Viola said. "It indicates you are honest. How much has Parthenium told you?"

Spencer glanced at Parthenium again, but she only smiled gently at him. "Enough to confuse me greatly."

"Do you believe everything she has told you?"

He thought about this. "I trust Parthenium. But I can't say I believe everything she has told me."

Viola took a sip of her blackberry cordial. "Would you like to believe everything she has told you?"

He sighed. "Mrs. Templeton, I feel like I'm being tested—like I'm back at Drury. Do you have a study guide or something I can have?"

Parthenium giggled, and then Viola smiled broadly.

Spencer looked from one to the other. "Are you guys messing with me?"

Still smiling, Viola said, "Don't you know girls have to fool people every day of their lives if they want to get anywhere?"

Spencer shook his head for lack of a better response. "Well, it's obvious you are Parthenium's mother."

Parthenium giggled even harder.

Viola said, "Yes, but what you really want to know is, who is Parthenium's father."

The laughing stopped.

"Ma'am, that's probably none of my—"

"It's Parthenium's time," Viola said. "Her year. And it's her choice what she does with it. Parthenium tells me she wants you to be a part of her time. Do you want to be a part of her time, Spencer?"

Spencer looked at Parthenium. Her eyes were confident, perhaps naive, as if she were not even aware of the possibility that he might say no.

He spoke without breaking his gaze with Parthenium. "Yes, ma'am, I do."

"Then let's start with what you don't believe," Viola said.

As if she knew what was coming next, Parthenium nodded to him slightly, granting him permission.

Spencer took a long breath and faced Viola. "Parthenium told me you go up to Johnson's Shut-Ins every year to visit the gravesite of your husband. And that when you come back you are pregnant. Ma'am, I think Parthenium believes her father is your husband, who died at least five years before she was born. And I also think she believes the same man is the father of all her siblings, even the youngest, Delphinium."

Viola studied him for a moment and Spencer prepared for the worst.

"She does believe that, Spencer." Her voice was still friendly.

"I'm not sure it's fair to let her believe it. Why not tell her who her father is?"

Viola took a long drink from her glass. "I was only five when I began to understand how different our family is. My parents avoided going into town, because of how people treated them. They were not sin eaters. My grandparents had been, but the last time they practiced it was in 1944. This didn't matter, though. The chains of habit are too weak to be felt until they are too strong to be broken. Scorning my family was a habit, and people continue it even now. During my life, I have cultivated within my children and myself an indifference to this scorn. And so, Spencer, I do not feel a need for you to believe what Parthenium has told you, or what I am about to tell you."

She paused and gazed down at her glass. "Twain said, 'Never tell the truth to people who are not worthy of it.' Parthenium tells me you are worthy, Spencer."

He made the effort to look her in the eye. "I hope so."

She took another drink. "Parthenium's father was a man like no other. And I love him like no other woman could. I will always love him. Nearly every July I have gone to the place where I had spread his ashes. Each time I came back, I was carrying a child. So nearly every April I bore another of his children. I did not go to see another man, as people often accused me of behind my back. I did not go to a doctor to have his preserved seed implanted in my ovaries. I went there to talk to him, to tell him I loved him still and how wonderful all his children have become.

"I don't know how I continued to bear his children. I have spent too many hours researching, looking for answers. Maybe it's something different about me. Did you know there are many animals in which the females store sperm in their bodies for years? Snakes and fish—even chickens do this. They continue to have offspring long after they mate with a male, even years after the male has died. Maybe that's what I can do." She paused as if giving him a chance to ask questions.

Spencer simply waited for her to go on.

"Or maybe there was residual ash from my husband's body at the place where I had scattered it, and somehow it entered my body when I went there, fertilizing my eggs. There was one summer I did not go there, and that year I did not become pregnant. I stopped going there three years ago and haven't become pregnant since. And there are still other possible explanations. But the simple fact of the matter is, I don't know how it happened. I just know it was a blessing. All my children are gifted in ways that never cease to surprise me. They did not inherit their gifts from me, as I am a plain and average woman. It is their father who has passed his gifts to them, as well as his curse."

Spencer frowned and looked at Parthenium. Her eyes became wide.

"No, Mother! This is not the time."

Viola drained the last of her blackberry cordial. "You don't believe that, Parthenium. Because you're a lover, like me, and you love Spencer. I can see that you do. And you know it *is* time."

Suddenly Spencer realized how surreal things had become. He stared at Parthenium. Tears were forming in her eyes.

Viola said, "You know it is, Parthenium."

Parthenium wiped her eyes and then nodded at her mother. She turned to Spencer. "She's right, I love you. And I'm sorry."

Spencer felt a wave of heat pass through him, which then turned to nausea. "What are you talking about?"

Viola set her glass down and stood up. "Come with me." She then left the room.

Without saying a word, Parthenium took Spencer's hand and they followed Viola out the front door and up the hill toward the stone school. The faces of Parthenium's brothers and sisters watched through the windows as they walked past the school and continued up the hill. Finally, they came to a clearing and stopped.

Spencer stared, struggling to process what was before him. In a row upon the ground were six stone markers. Stark and simplistic, each of them had only a first name carved into the stone. Spencer looked at the first marker on the left. It said Cirsium. The one next to it said Iris. Next to that, Tamias. And then Dalea, Trillium, and Mertensia.

Parthenium and her mother remained silent, waiting.

"I don't understand," Spencer said. He barely heard himself speak, his blood gushing in his ears with every heartbeat.

Viola took his elbow in her hand before speaking to him. "My husband, Victor Dailey, was an exceptional man. A gifted man. But as with many gifts of the mind, there were side effects. He died just after his twenty-first birthday." She then paused as if she were uncertain Spencer understood her.

"He just died," she said. "No one knew why. But whatever the cause, it is an inherited trait. My first daughter, Cirsium, passed away a week after her twenty-first birthday. Iris passed away two weeks before her twenty-first. And then a year later, my son Tamias. A year later, Dalea, and a year after that, Trillium. And just two months ago, four days before her twenty-first birthday, Mertensia passed."

Spencer couldn't speak. He turned to look at Parthenium.

"I'm sorry," she sobbed. "I should have told you."

He went to her and embraced her. And he kissed her for the first time.

SEPTEMBER

Spencer was in decent shape. Since high school, he had been running three times per week, usually a mile or two. But Parthenium was in a totally different class. They were less than halfway around the two-mile loop and she had already paused to wait for him.

He stopped beside her and put his hands on his knees to catch his breath. It didn't help that the trail climbed and descended several hills as it wound its way around the perimeter of the Templeton property.

"I'm sorry," he panted. "You're a natural. I'm not." He then almost said something about how he wished he had her running genes but then decided any comment on her inherited traits might seem crass.

She waited patiently for his breathing to even out before speaking. "I don't think I've ever told you why I chose running as a specialty subject."

Spencer looked up at her and just shook his head.

"It was because of Tamias. I was eleven, he was fourteen. He loved to run, although he never went so far as to declare it a specialty subject. This was years before Cirsium died, so we had no idea what was coming. There wasn't as much pressure then to narrow our focus to only one subject. My younger siblings now, they don't waste their time on anything else."

"No kidding," Spencer said. He had seen this. The kids were all brilliant, but they were so determined to make an impact on the world during their twenty-first year that they had no interests beyond their chosen specialties.

"You ready?" she asked.

When Spencer nodded, they both jogged at a pace that would allow them to talk.

"Tamias let me run with him, but I could never keep up. We would run this course every day. Again and again, he would finish the course two or three minutes before me. My siblings aren't the type who let you win for the sake of your self-esteem." She gave Spencer a sidelong glance, smiling slightly.

He spoke between breaths. "As you've said, you're not like your brothers or sisters."

She went on. "Finally I got discouraged. Actually, I got mad. I told Tamias I wasn't running with him anymore because I would never be able to keep up. I was done with running. The next day, when he was ready to run, he came and found me and made me put on my running clothes and shoes. We went to the trailhead, and he said, 'Parthenium, why can't you keep up with me when we run?' I told him I couldn't go any faster because it hurt too much. He said, 'What if you thought about pain differently? What if you believed pain was a gift, a gift that was given to you every time you tried to do something great, something you've never been able to do before?' He then turned and ran off, leaving me there to think about that. I ran up the trail. I didn't catch him that day, of course, or for many days after that. But I began to appreciate the gift of pain."

Apparently the story was over.

"Eventually you beat him, I guess?"

She glanced at him with a smile but remained silent.

"I have a story for you," he said. "When I was a kid I grabbed a big, hairy wolf spider because I had no idea what it was. It bit my finger, and it hurt like h—, well it hurt a lot. So I don't go around now looking for wolf spiders to grab. That would be, like, stupid."

She smiled at him again and then sped up, leaving him behind.

"Goddammit," he muttered, and then he poured it on, trying to catch her.

He was only fifty yards behind her when they arrived at the trailhead next to the house. He nearly doubled over trying to breathe.

"A few fly bites cannot stop a spirited horse," she said to him.

He nodded. "Another month. Then I'll beat you."

"That's what I like to hear. I need two more laps. You'll be okay here, won't you?"

He waved his hand dismissively. "I'll time you." He sat on one of the chairs next to the covered control panel, pressed a blue Reset button, and held his finger over a green Start button. He nodded at her and then pressed the button when she took off. The course was exactly two miles, with motion sensors mounted on the trail every quarter mile so they could record and analyze her split times.

"I expect you have some news for me." Parthenium's mom took a seat next to Spencer.

Spencer turned to face Viola. How would she react to what he had to say? He studied her face for a moment. At only forty-three, she had given birth to twenty-three children and had already lost six of them. Perhaps it was only because Spencer knew these things, but her eyes seemed to reveal a lifetime's worth of joy as well as an unthinkable level of sorrow.

"Yes, I do," he said. "Hold on a second." He walked to his Malibu and retrieved a folded sheet of paper from the front dash. As he leaned into the car he looked at the four bottles of water he had put in the back seat. One of the 7-gallon plastic bottles had fallen onto its side, so he pushed it upright. He took the folded paper back to Viola.

"It's from the County Extension Office," he said as he handed it to her. "You can look it over, but I'll summarize what I know. They recommended I talk to a Dr. Randall Cleves in Poplar Bluff. So I drove up there and he went over the report with me."

Spencer glanced at the control panel and saw the second in a row of eight runner-shaped icons turn green. Parthenium had just completed the first half-mile in two minutes and forty seconds. Viola had stopped looking at the paper and was gazing at him, waiting.

He sat next to her. "Viola, they recommend having any drinking water source tested every year. You've never had your spring water tested?"

She shook her head.

"Dr. Cleves pointed out two important findings," he said. "First, your spring water has a higher than normal level of arsenic." He noted her look of alarm and quickly added, "The level isn't extremely high, but high enough that there could possibly be some concern if you were to exclusively drink this water over a long period of time—like decades." Her look of alarm did not improve. "He explained to me that arsenic gets into the water because it gradually dissolves out of certain rock formations. So this level of arsenic has probably always been in your spring."

"My family has been drinking this water for generations," she said. "If the water has anything to do with my children dying, there would have to be something in it that is more recent. This didn't happen before Parthenium's generation."

Spencer nodded. "The other important finding is that the nitrite and nitrate levels are high. This is much more likely to have happened recently. As with the arsenic, the levels of nitrite and nitrate aren't high enough to be drastically alarming. I asked Dr. Cleves if there was anything about these contaminant levels that could be dangerous, that might even kill people." Spencer leaned forward, resting his elbows on his knees, and added, "As you requested, I didn't tell him your secret, even though he wanted to know if I had a specific reason for asking such a question. He studied the results for a while and then explained that often these kinds of contaminants, arsenic especially, are known to interact with each other, causing unusual or amplified effects. Arsenic has even been known to interact specifically with nitrites and nitrates. So it's possible these have increased in recent years for some reason and have modified the effects of arsenic." He looked directly at her. "Viola, there is quite a bit of evidence that exposure to arsenic during childhood can increase mortality in young adults."

She gazed back at him with hollow and haunted eyes. "What causes nitrite and nitrate levels to increase?"

"That was my next question. Sometimes it's from agricultural runoff." He waved his hand at the surrounding forest. "That's not much of a possibility here. It's also caused by waste from animals, or by the decaying of large amounts of organic matter."

Her eyes became wide.

"What, Viola?"

She looked down at her lap. "When I moved back home after Victor died, my mother and father were not making many sin swallowers, so I took over that task. That was the year Cirsium was born. The sin swallowers made with fish bones were the most popular by far, but there were only so many fish in our spring. I needed more. I introduced trout into the spring and began feeding them food pellets. Before long I had as many trout as I needed." She looked up at him. "There are a lot of trout in the spring. A lot."

"That many fish would create quite a bit of waste," he said.

She nodded. "And many of the pellets go uneaten, sinking to the bottom to decay." She looked back down at her lap. "If I had known they were going to do this," she said with a soft voice, "I would have become a shoemaker."

Spencer raised his brows in puzzlement. "Viola?"

"Einstein said that," she replied.

He put a hand on one of hers. "There's no point in blaming yourself for anything. Nothing about this is certain. In fact, since your kids haven't shown progressive symptoms, it's probably a long shot. But I came out today to request something—to beg you if I have to. Could you please have your family stop drinking spring water? I brought four bottles of drinking water to get you started. And I'll keep bringing as much as you need, although I may need your help paying for it."

Viola nodded slightly, apparently giving consent.

At that moment, Parthenium ran by them. She smiled but was breathing too hard to speak. Spencer glanced at the control panel. Ten minutes and nineteen seconds.

"Good God!"

"Parthenium's a runner," Viola said. "And an artist, and a singer. But mostly she's a lover. You're a good person, Spencer, and I'm happy you're here for her in her year."

"Maybe we'll have more time than just this year."

She smiled at this, but her face betrayed her doubts. "For five years I have believed this to be an inherited trait from my husband. Perhaps I have found some comfort in that belief, as it is a way to relieve myself of the blame. Of course, I hope you are right, Spencer, but if it turns out that my children are dying because of something I have done—something I could have stopped doing years ago…" She ended this thought by shaking her head.

"You can't blame yourself for any of this."

She half-smiled. "We gather our arms full of guilt as though it were precious stuff. It must be that we want it that way." She then leaned forward with her elbows on her knees. "This is not for Parthenium's ears."

Spencer frowned and nodded.

"A few months after Tamias died—he was the third to go—I realized what was happening, and I stopped going to my husband's gravesite. Therefore I stopped birthing children." She paused and looked up at the trees, their leaves just starting to turn. She blinked a few times as if holding back tears. "At that time I started to truly understand that for every good thing in the world, there is an evil thing fighting to even the score. For the holy force that blessed me with Victor's children, there was bound to be a maligned force determined to take them away. Good versus evil, God versus Satan, or maybe Nature simply made a mistake and she's trying to fix it—it doesn't really matter. They're all dying, and I have to watch them go, one at a time. I have to because until the day the last one has gone, they need me, and I need them."

She looked down the running trail and then back at Spencer. "But when that day comes, when the last of them—my sweet Delphinium—has passed beyond, I will not endure even one more hour of my suffering."

There was a moment of silence. "What are you saying, Viola?"

"I'm saying it will be time, after devoting myself to my beloved children, to at last do one self-indulgent and merciful thing for myself. But don't miss the main point of my story."

"Which is?"

"If there is one—even just one—person in the world who loves you, rejoice in it and give yourself to her."

It was Spencer's turn to glance down the trail. "I love Parthenium more than I ever thought possible. I'm not going anywhere."

Viola smiled at him. "Like I said, you're a good person. Parthenium is so happy right now, at a time when most people would drown in self-pity."

They sat in silence for a few minutes.

"I force my children to stay on the property until they are twenty. I'll admit I'm guilty of that. But I want you to know I don't force them to achieve something great during their year. Cirsium and Iris set a standard of excellence, and the younger ones then put the pressure on themselves to make their mark on the world."

Spencer looked up as Parthenium sprinted down the trail and crossed the line. The timer said 10:13—faster than the previous lap. "I certainly can believe that, ma'am."

∞

An hour later Spencer had carried the four water bottles to the house, and he and Parthenium had changed out of their running clothes. Spencer and Viola told Parthenium about the water test results and she agreed to help convince her younger siblings to stop drinking the spring water.

After they positioned one of the water bottles onto the dispenser base, Parthenium filled a glass and took a drink. She made a disapproving face. "I suppose we could get used to it."

Viola took the glass of water, drank some herself, and made a similar face. "The right choice is hardly ever the easy choice," she said.

Parthenium took Spencer's hand in hers. "I have two presents for you today!" She then led him to the door.

They walked up the hill and entered the stone school, where Parthenium's sixteen remaining sisters and brothers were busy with their projects and lessons. The place was like no school Spencer had seen before. The kids wandered from room to room at will, working on whatever activities interested them at the moment and often helping teach and care for their younger siblings. Every room was cluttered with haphazard clusters of desks and chairs, tablets and computers, instruments and recording equipment, video and still cameras, ovens and cooking supplies, tools and building materials, and piles of papers and books. The Templeton kids could explore any interest and develop any skill. It was both stimulating and chaotic.

As soon as they entered the school, shouts and hugs from a half dozen of the younger kids greeted Spencer. As they made their way to the stairs, Ursus bounded out of a doorway with a loud growl. Spencer responded by growling back at him with his hands raised like claws, a ritual that had developed because Ursus was named for the Missouri black bear. The boys were all named for mammals, the girls for wildflowers.

They climbed the stairs to the second floor, and Spencer paused by the first door and stuck his head in. "How's the app coming, Lotus?"

She sat with her back to him, facing four large computer monitors arranged in a semicircle before her. Without turning around, Lotus said, "Morning, Spencer. A little closer every day. At least I got the GPS interface issue figured out."

Spencer looked at the two monitors that were currently turned on. One displayed a detailed aerial-view map, and the other was filled with rows of indecipherable code. Lotus was developing an app to guide people to historical sites, natural landmarks, and other points of interest in the Ozark region of the Midwest. She was fifteen.

Parthenium led Spencer to the corner room where she pursued her second specialty subject, Ozark folk art. The room was nearly filled with tables upon which were various works in progress, several computers, books left open on certain pages, and hundreds of clear plastic boxes filled with supplies such as bones, dried flowers, and feathers. These were arranged by size, shape, and color. Numerous completed works hung on the walls, perhaps half of them sin swallowers.

Upon entering the room, Parthenium became visibly excited. She went to one of the interior walls where a sheet with faded red and white stripes concealed a large circular object.

"I wanted to create something new, just for you," she said, nearly giggling with anticipation. "You already have a sin swallower, so I decided to make you something that is kind of the opposite of that." She carefully removed the striped cloth.

Spencer expected the object to be beautiful, but he didn't expect it to be mesmerizing. It was round, perhaps eighteen inches in diameter, and made mostly of feathers. The feathers were arranged in spirals, reminding him somewhat of the dragonfly-wing creation she had given him, but this was much larger and was not transparent.

"They're wood duck feathers," she said. "For now I'm calling it a love illuminator. I know it's silly, but so is a sin swallower, right? Here's my idea. You hang it on your wall, and instead of swallowing your sins, it illuminates your love for other people. When someone looks at it, if they look at it just right, they will see how much love you have for them." She took his arm and guided him over so that he was standing directly in front of it. "You have to try it, Spencer! Look right at the middle of it. If you don't see anything interesting after a minute or so, that means I don't have much love for you. The more interesting and beautiful it appears to you, the more love I have for you."

He smiled and shook his head. "I already know you love me."

"You have to try it!"

He planted his feet firmly and stared at the center of the spiraling feathers. The room became silent as Parthenium waited. For some seconds he simply appraised the thing's intricate beauty. But suddenly, as he stared directly at the center of it, the layered spirals seemed to spin, an optical illusion. He watched it, fascinated, as the spinning motion accelerated. Suddenly the brighter feathers, which until now he'd thought were placed randomly, began to move. They converged toward the center and then expanded again, in alternating spirals of green, blue, and white. Spencer squeezed his eyes shut, hardly believing what he had seen. When he opened them again, the illusion of movement had stopped. But as he stared at the feathers, his eyes went slightly out of focus, and the apparent movement began all over again, the spirals of color collapsing and expanding one after another.

"Spencer?"

Reluctantly, he took his eyes off the object to look at Parthenium. "This might be the most beautiful thing I've ever seen."

She looked very pleased. "You see? It *is* a love illuminator. It has shown you how much love I have for you."

He shook his head. "You're amazing. You started with a pile of feathers, and somehow you made this."

She smiled. "A rock pile ceases to be a rock pile the moment a single man contemplates it, bearing within him the image of a cathedral." She then waved her hand at the items arranged in disarray on the tables. "Folk art has been one of my specialty subjects since I was five. With enough time and determination, anyone can make beautiful things—or even touch the stars."

Spencer stepped up to the love illuminator to study it closely. "I'm not so sure about that," he said. He then pulled out his smartphone and began taking photos of it.

Parthenium said, "I don't know why you bother taking pictures of all these pieces. They don't really work the way they're supposed to unless you have the real piece in front of you."

He glanced at her between photos. "You have your specialty subjects, I have mine." Finally, he put the phone back in his pocket and stepped back to admire the object again. Within seconds the illusion of movement began and he watched the lines of color shrink and grow.

"Okay, I can't wait any longer," she said. "I have another present for you."

With some effort, Spencer pulled his gaze from the love illuminator and followed her to another corner room of the second floor, the music studio. She turned on a few pieces of equipment and then tapped a microphone, which responded with a deep thump.

"I have a new song! I wrote this one myself. It's your other present."

This was a surprise. As far as Spencer knew, Parthenium had not been particularly interested in composing her own songs. "You wrote a song for me? Hold on, then." He turned on the digital mixer and checked the mic connection. "Will you use your guitar?"

"It's a cappella," she said. "But you really don't need to record it."

He smiled. "You wrote a song for me. I absolutely need to record it." He pressed a button to start recording.

She rolled her eyes. "It's in the style of an Ozark folk song. Sorry, that's just what I know best. It's called *Twenty-one Years*." She then began singing.

PARTHENIUM'S YEAR

Come all you young lovers,
And listen awhile to me,
A bittersweet story,
And a girl's final plea.

A kind old mother, have I,
As kind as she can be,
She always shares my troubles,
And often agrees with me.

My sisters and my brothers,
They love me night and day,
Wanting and needful am I,
Giving and bounteous are they.

But my siblings bear a burden,
And sadly, so do I,
For after twenty-one years,
We quickly fade and die.

Now a man named Spencer Wolfe,
Has claimed my cursed heart,
And I have claimed his,
Although we soon must part.

So come all you young lovers,
And listen awhile to me,
A bittersweet story,
And a girl's final plea.

Live the moments of your life,
As if each were your last,
For one day you'll awaken,
To find your moments passed.

> Find and love another,
> As if there were no other,
> For one day you'll awaken,
> To find that they've been taken.
>
> Now I'm in my twenty-first year,
> My moments are not long,
> You may forget the singer,
> But don't forget her song.

After a long moment of silence, Spencer realized the song was finished. He pressed a button on the mixer to stop recording. He wiped his eyes and waited until he could speak.

"I don't really understand what's happening," he managed to choke out. He should have waited a little longer. "There's nothing special about me. I was just a guy, trying to figure out what to do with my life. And now I'm here with you. There is no possible way in this universe that I deserve to be loved by someone as magical as you, Parthenium." He wiped his eyes again. "I feel like I don't have anything to offer you."

She rushed over and embraced him, pressing her forehead into his neck. "You don't understand. You are you. That is truer than true. There is no one alive who is youer than you."

He pulled back and looked her in the eye. "At this moment, Dr. Suess?"

She laughed. "It seemed appropriate. But you really don't understand, Spencer. You are my year. You. Not someone else. To me, that is everything. Sure, I can run, and sing, and make art. But with three specialty subjects, I never became good enough at any of them to really accomplish something in my year. But then you came into my life, and I realized my mother was right all along.

Running isn't my specialty subject, nor is music or art. I am a lover."

She gazed at him in a way that no one had ever done before.

"Spencer, in this story, I am the poet, you are the poetry."

APRIL

Spencer stared at the 3D model on his computer monitor. It was an interactive image of the first gift Parthenium had given him, the circular array of dragonfly wings with a lens at the center. He put his finger on the screen and moved it in a circle. The model rotated in response, distorting the photo of a tree he had selected for the background focal point. It worked perfectly, just as he had requested. He had contracted a graphic designer to have the model created. The cost of this hadn't been a problem—Viola had paid for it—but Spencer had needed to drive the delicate object, along with fifteen others, over to Rolla to be photographed by the designers. He hadn't been willing to risk shipping them. But now, as he inspected each 3D model, it became obvious it was worth the effort.

A familiar ringtone broke his concentration and he snatched up his cell phone. "Doing okay, Parthenium?"

"Well, I just set a personal record on the trail, so I must still be alive."

"Congratulations! 10:02?"

"Ten even, plus a few hundredths. I wish you could have stayed longer, Spencer." Her voice was pleading, perhaps even frightened.

"I'll come first thing in the morning, I swear. I just really wanted to wrap a few things up here." What he didn't say was that he was trying to finish the project while she was still alive to see it. It was *his* gift to her.

"Will you be here before I wake up?" Spencer glanced at the clock. It was already 10:00 pm. "I'll try. Call me if anything happens, okay?"

"I'm sure nothing will happen, my love, but you know I will."

"Parthenium?"

"Yes?"

"Tell me a story about courage, okay?"

"Courage?" She hesitated for a moment. "When my mother was a girl—before she met my father—she was adventurous, a tomboy. Is that a word people use?"

"Tomboy? Yes."

"She would run wild all over the woods, even off our property all the way to Coon Island Conservation Area. Back then Coon Island wasn't flooded like it is now. She had favorite places where she would sit and read. One of them was on a bluff looking over the Black River. She had to climb the rocks to get to her sitting spot. Thirty feet high, if you ask her now, although I remember when she used to say it was twenty."

"You're going to tell me she fell, aren't you?"

"Do you want to hear my story, or would you rather just guess what's going to happen?"

Spencer chuckled. "Go on."

"As it turns out, she did fall. All the way to the rocks on the river bank. She tried to land on her feet but broke both knees and an ankle. Three miles from home. My grandparents didn't know where she was. They didn't even know she was gone until supper time. No one was around to hear her calling for help, and eventually it got dark. My mother had no choice but to lay there on the rocks by the river."

"That sounds horrible."

"It was a long night for her. She believed she was going to die. She was afraid, and she cried most of the night. In the morning, a man who was hunting turkeys heard her calling for help. He carried her out of the woods to his truck. Try to imagine what it took to endure that. He drove her to the hospital in Poplar Bluff. When they arrived, the man told my mother she was the bravest person he had ever met. And he was a Vietnam veteran."

Parthenium fell silent.

"Your mother *is* brave," Spencer said.

"But that's the irony of it. She wasn't brave at all that night. She was terrified. But after all those hours of darkness and torment, she was still calling for help in the morning. Teddy Roosevelt said, 'Courage is not having the strength to go on; it is going on when you don't have the strength.'"

They both remained silent for several long seconds.

"You're brave like your mother," he said.

"No. You can't be brave if you've only had wonderful things happen to you."

He nodded and then realized she couldn't see him.

After they hung up, Spencer stared at the 3D model on his screen. The night ahead of him would be too short and too long. It was too short to finish his book, and it was too long to be away from Parthenium. Her twenty-first birthday was a week ago. Three of her older siblings had passed before their birthdays, three of them after, but all of them within a few weeks. It could happen at any time. Or maybe it wouldn't happen at all.

There was a knock on his bedroom door. "Come on in, Mom."

She entered and put a fresh cup of coffee on his desk.

"I've been home a year," he said, "you can stop waiting on me."

PARTHENIUM'S YEAR

Instead of responding, she watched over his shoulder as he continued spinning the model. "When are you going to tell Parthenium about the book?"

This was a question she had asked several times before. Spencer had not yet told his mom all he knew about the Templeton family, particularly the part about the kids dying every year in April. He just couldn't think of a way to tell her without initiating something. He didn't know what it would be, but it would be something unpleasant. She would know soon enough, or she wouldn't.

"It's a surprise for her," he said.

She sighed and sat at the edge of the bed, a sign that he should turn around and talk to her. He took a drink from the mug, swiveled around, and forced a smile.

"I'm supportive of this, Spence. I am." She then nodded toward the computers and cameras on the desk behind him. "And obviously Viola supports it. But when I ask you about it, you blow it off, like you're hiding something or don't want to bother. You've been home, living in my house, almost a year without looking for a job." She raised her hands to prevent him from responding. "And that's fine! If you believe in this, so do I. But don't I deserve to know more about it?"

He gazed at her, and his fake smile gradually became real. He glanced at the clock again. "You're right. I should have told you more about this." He grabbed a chair from the corner and dragged it over for her to sit in. He then opened the partially completed ebook and displayed the title on his screen: PARTHENIUM'S YEAR—HOW TO LIVE AND LOVE LIKE EVERY YEAR IS YOUR LAST.

Her brows furrowed as she read the title. "What does that mean, Spencer?"

"I promise I'll explain it to you soon. Then it will make sense. But I just can't right now. It would take too long. Is that okay?"

She nodded, but lines of concern creased her face.

He flipped to the table of contents. "It's basically a book for anyone seeking inspiration. It's filled with stories, quotes, and multimedia in four sections: running, Ozark folk music, folk art, and most important, how to love unselfishly. What I hope makes it unique is that it is interactive. It has 3D models the reader can manipulate, as well as recorded songs readers can listen to and learn to play themselves. There is guidance for singing and playing instruments."

She stared at the screen as he flipped through the content. "You really love her, don't you Spence?"

He snorted a brief laugh. "That's kind of an understatement."

"I'm happy for you, son. I really am. But I'm compelled to ask a practical question, a question about the entrepreneurial aspect of this. I know everything in this book is important to you, but why would other people care about some girl they don't know living in rural Missouri? What makes you think people will buy this book?"

Spencer smiled broadly. "Are you forgetting that I have a specialty subject? You paid for most of my marketing degree, and I have no intention of wasting it." He opened the web browser on his computer. The home page that came up was a blog. It was titled, *What's In A Name?*

"This is my blog," he said. "A few times per week I write about Parthenium—what she says, what she does, how these things affect me." He then turned and looked at her. "Want to know how many readers I have?"

"How many?"

He opened an administrative screen for the blog and pointed to a number.

"Sweet Jesus! Over a million? How is that possible?"

"You'd be surprised what you can do with a few ads here, and a few guest blogs there. And most of all, by writing from the heart. Mom, every one of those readers knows my book will be ready soon, and by surveying them I know most of them intend to buy it."

She shook her head. "A million?"

"That's the purpose of the blog in the first place—to build a strong base of readers who will eventually buy the book. And they'll tell others to buy it." He leaned toward her and took her hands in his. "Parthenium wanted to make the world a better place. I'm helping her do that. But this has taken longer than I intended. I'm out of time."

She gazed at him, her face still lined with concern. "You think she's going to die, don't you? Like those two sisters of hers."

He looked down at her hands, which were gripping his. They were starting to show dark splotches of age. How lucky she was to have such hands.

"I hope she doesn't," he said. When he looked back up at her face, he saw pain in her eyes. She was hurting for him. It was not unlike the haunting sorrow he saw every day in the eyes of Viola Templeton.

"Read to me, Spence," she said. "I'd like you to read something to me that a million people think is worth reading."

He smiled, released her hands, and turned back to the computer. "I'll read you my most recent post." He clicked out of the administrative screen.

Parthenium has turned twenty-one—ten months and twelve days after telling me her name. Every day since then has been a gift. That is how I like to think of birthdays. We give people gifts on their birthdays, and I like to think this is our way of saying thank you—thank you for being alive and enriching my life for the past year.

On her birthday, Parthenium told me a story. As many of her stories are, it was of a seemingly innocuous event from her childhood. She was fishing for trout with her mother. She was a young girl and had not been fishing before. Soon her mother caught a large trout. She carried the trout to a wide wooden box her family had constructed near the spring. She placed the fish on the box's lid and said, 'Parthenium, let's name this fish Clematis. Do you want to say thank you to Clematis?'

Parthenium asked her mother why she wanted her to thank the fish.

Her mother explained that the fish was giving them its bones, which they would use to craft the product that was the centerpiece of their family's business. Indeed, the fish was giving its very life.

Parthenium then asked why her mother would want to give the fish a name if she was just going to kill it anyway.

Her mother told her that when you know someone's name, you can have feelings for them. You can love them.

'Why would you want to love a fish that is going to die?' Parthenium asked.

Her mother said, 'I love Clematis because this fish is giving us a gift. In fact, it is giving us everything it has.'

Parthenium looked at the fish and said, 'Thank you, Clematis.'

Her mother took an ice pick that hung from the box by a cord and pushed it into one side of the fish's head until the point came out the other. She then raised the box's lid and dropped the trout into the box, which was full of sawdust and dermestid beetles. The beetles would soon consume its flesh, leaving behind perfect, white bones.

I've been thinking lately about gifts. I am one of those people who finds gift giving to be awkward. I never seem to know what to give people. And the gifts I give are often laughably off the mark. One time I was at an event and as a door prize, I won a gift certificate for a romantic night out for two. I had no use for it, so I gave it to my mom for her birthday. The problem was, she and my dad had divorced years before, and she had no interest in dating other men. She laughed at the gift and then informed me that I would have to be her date. How comfortable do you think that was for a less-than-confident 17-year-old? Another time, when I was even younger, I had an incurable crush on the older sister of my friend, Ben. I was invited to Ben's 11th birthday party. For a gift, I selected the third book in the series, *The Sisterhood of the Traveling Pants*. Why? Because I had observed Ben's older sister reading these books, and I thought she might be impressed by my taste in literature. She was not even present at the birthday party. How much appreciation do you think Ben had for my gift?

It is time I learned the art of giving gifts, and Parthenium is my teacher. She takes gift giving to a new level. Her gifts do not cost a lot of money. Most of them, in fact, cost nothing but time, effort, and boundless creativity.

One day, after I had told her of my gift giving disability, she said to me, 'A wise lover values not so much the gift of the lover as the love of the giver.' The next day I looked this up and discovered it was a quote from Thomas á Kempis, from a book he wrote in the 1420s called The Imitation of Christ. This book was a guide for renouncing worldly vanities and finding eternal truths. How steadfastly appropriate.

Perhaps I can give a small gift to my lover by telling you, my readers, something I'd like you to remember:

Her name is Parthenium.

Spencer saw a reflection of movement on his computer screen—his mom lifting a hand to wipe her eyes. He sat in silence with his back to her for several long minutes. Finally, she stood up, kissed the top of his head, and left him alone with his work.

Later that night, at 3:18 AM, Spencer got a call from Viola Templeton.

Author's Notes

Parthenium's Year is dedicated to my wife, my parents, my siblings, my aunts and uncles, and my children, without whom I would not know the true power of love.

Quotes used in Parthenium's Year:

"What's in a name? that which we call a rose. By any other name would smell as sweet."
— William Shakespeare

"Kiss a lover
Dance a measure,
Find your name
And buried treasure..."
- Neil Gaiman, The Graveyard Book

"Fear doesn't shut you down; it wakes you up."
— Veronica Roth, Divergent

"Conversations consist for the most part of things one does not say."
— Cees Nooteboom

"For so many centuries, the exchange of gifts has held us together. It has made it possible to bridge the abyss where language struggles."
— Barry López, About This Life

"Story is a butterfly whose wings transport us to another world where we receive gifts that change who we are and who we want to be."
— Harley King

PARTHENIUM'S YEAR

"When people will not weed their own minds, they are apt to be overrun by nettles."
— Horace Walpole

"So do all who live to see such times. But that is not for them to decide. All we have to decide is what to do with the time that is given us."
— J.R.R. Tolkien, The Fellowship of the Ring

"I'm in no hurry: the sun and the moon aren't, either. Nobody goes faster than the legs they have.
— Alberto Caeiro, The Collected Poems of Alberto Caeiro

"How soon hath Time, the subtle thief of youth,
Stol'n on his wing my three-and-twentieth year!"
— John Milton

"Time is too slow for those who wait, too swift for those who fear, too long for those who grieve, too short for those who rejoice, but for those who love, time is eternity."
— Henry Van Dyke

"Not only is the Universe stranger than we think, it is stranger than we can think."
— Werner Heisenberg, Across the Frontiers

"I have noticed that the people who are late are often so much jollier than the people who have to wait for them."
— Edward Verrall Lucas

"Don't you know girls have to fool people every day of their lives if they want to get anywhere?"
— Salman Rushdie, Haroun and the Sea of Stories

Stan C. Smith

"The chains of habit are too weak to be felt until they are too strong to be broken."
— Samuel Johnson

"A few fly bites cannot stop a spirited horse."
— Mark Twain

"If I had known they were going to do this, I would have become a shoemaker."
— Albert Einstein

"We gather our arms full of guilt as though it were precious stuff. It must be that we want it that way."
— John Steinbeck

"The right choice is hardly ever the easy choice."
— Rick Riordan, The Throne of Fire

"A rock pile ceases to be a rock pile the moment a single man contemplates it, bearing within him the image of a cathedral."
— Antoine de Saint-Exupéry, The Little Prince

"Today you are You, that is truer than true. There is no one alive who is Youer than You."
— Dr. Seuss, Happy Birthday to You!

"In this story, I am the poet, you're the poetry."
— Arzum Uzun

"Courage is not having the strength to go on; it is going on when you don't have the strength."
— Theodore Roosevelt

PARTHENIUM'S YEAR

"You can't be brave if you've only had wonderful things happen to you."
— Mary Tyler Moore

"A wise lover values not so much the gift of the lover as the love of the giver."
— Thomas à Kempis, The Imitation of Christ

Stan C. Smith

Acknowledgements

Thanks to the University of Arkansas. Their University Libraries includes an amazing digital collection of traditional Ozark folk songs, the source of two of the songs in this story: *Adam Never Had No Dear Old Mammy* and *Autumn Leaves*.

http://digitalcollections.uark.edu/cdm/search/collection/OzarkFolkSong

These lyrics were used with permission from the University of Arkansas Libraries.

Of course, Parthenium Templeton composed the song, *Twenty-one Years*.

PARTHENIUM'S YEAR

About the Author

Stan Smith has lived most of his life in the Midwest United States and currently resides in Warrensburg, Missouri. He writes adventure novels and short stories that have a generous sprinkling of science fiction. His novels and stories are about regular people who find themselves caught up in highly unusual situations. They are designed to stimulate your sense of wonder, get your heart pounding, and keep you reading late into the night, with minimal risk of exposure to spelling and punctuation errors. His books are for anyone who loves adventure, discovery, and mind-bending surprises.

Stan's Author Website
http://www.stancsmith.com

Feel free to email Stan at: stan@stancsmith.com

He loves hearing from readers and will answer every email.

Also by Stan C. Smith

Have you read the entire Diffusion series?

Savage

If you have found this book, the end of the world has already begun.

Discover how it all started. In 1868, Samuel Inwood tragically stumbles upon the most significant discovery in human history, the Lamotelokhai. His story is one of wonder, survival, and gradual realization of the state of human civilization. And it is a warning to all of us….

Blue Arrow

Is the world ready for Peter Wooley?

Rose Wooley is in love. But her husband Peter is addicted to near-suicidal feats of endurance and adventure. Just when Rose can no longer bear the distress and heartache of his exploits, Peter returns from a trek through the remote wilderness of New Guinea. He claims that he will never leave her again, that he is now a new man. What Rose doesn't realize is how true this really is.

PARTHENIUM'S YEAR

Diffusion

What would you sacrifice to bring to light the greatest discovery in human history?

It's been 150 years since Samuel discovered the Lamotelokhai. Quentin Darnell and his group tragically become stranded in remote Papua. Soon they realize they aren't alone.

Infusion

Who would you trust with the power to alter the destiny of humanity?

Quentin and his group struggle to return to civilization. But transporting the greatest discovery in history is not as easy as it might seem.

Profusion

How can you save humanity if your only hope is to call upon the entity that could destroy us all?

Quentin and Lindsey take off for Papua in hopes of finding their lost son. One the other side of the world, Bobby and the Lamotelokhai find themselves locked in a struggle to save civilization.

For more information on these novels, as well as updates about new releases and exclusive promotions, visit the author's website and join his email newsletter at:

http://www.stancsmith.com

You may forget the singer,
but don't forget her song.

Made in the USA
Monee, IL
19 December 2019